Within the pages of this book
You may discover, if you look
Beyond the spell of written words,
A hidden land of beasts and birds.

For many things are 'of a kind',
And those with keenest eyes will find
A thousand things, or maybe more —
It's up to you to keep the score.

A final word before we go;
There's one more thing you ought to know:
In Animalia, you see,
It's possible you might find *me*.

— Graeme

For Robyn

Puffin Books

An Armoured Armadillo
Avoiding An
Angry
Alligator
ABCDE
FGHIJ
KLMNO
PQRST
UVWXY
Z
AMBULANCE
ATOM
BRAND
12

Beautiful
BLUE
BUTTERFLIES
basking
by a
BABBLING
BROOK

catching Crusty Crayfish
APRIL
CORN

DIABOLICAL
DRAGONS
DAINTILY DEVOURING
DELICIOUS
DELICACIES
DICTIONARY

BACHELOR OF MEDICINE
DIPLOMA OF DESIGN
Deluxe
12.5
6th JUNE 1944
1 Thou shalt
2. Thou shalt

EIGHT
ENORMOUS
ELEPHANTS
EXPERTLY EATING
EASTER EGGS
ENTRY
Emily
Ernest
ERIC
Ethel
ELIZABETH
Edw

FOUR
FAT
FROGS
FISHING
-FOR-
FRIGHTENED
FISH

GREAT GREEN GORILLAS
GROWING GRAPES IN A
GORGEOUS GLASS GREENHOUSE

Horrible
hairy
hogs
hurryin
home
~war
on
heavily
harnessed
horses

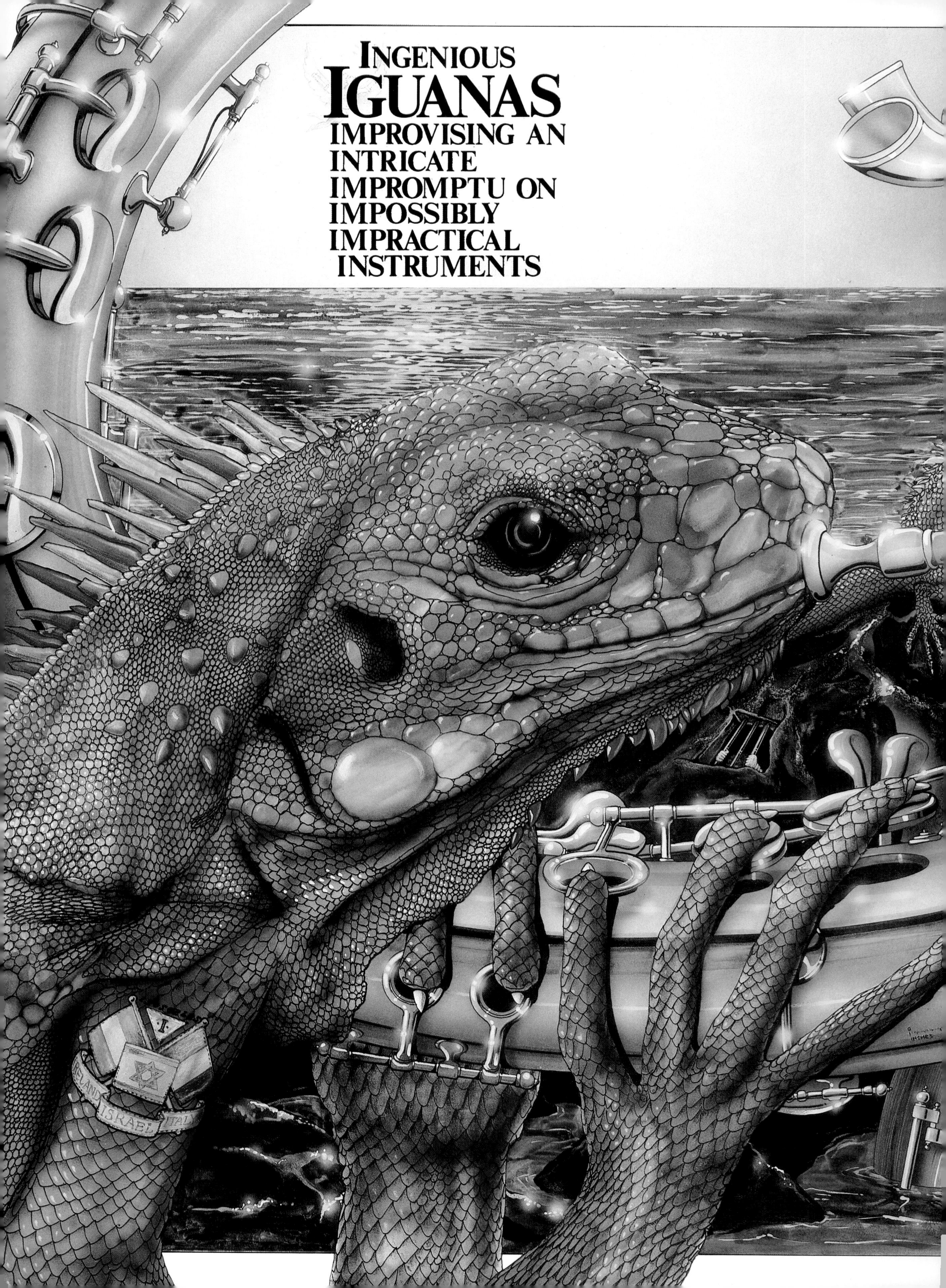
INGENIOUS
IGUANAS
IMPROVISING AN
INTRICATE
IMPROMPTU ON
IMPOSSIBLY
IMPRACTICAL
INSTRUMENTS
ISRAEL

IBIS
INSTRUMENTS
INC.
INDIAN
INK

· JOVIAL · JACKALS · JUGGLING · JUGS · OF · JELLY · IN · THE · JUNGLE ·

KID KOOKABURRA
and
KELLY KANGAROO
kidnapping
KITTY KOALA
KING ST.
The
ALEIDOSCOPE
KLUB
KIOSK
DOWNSTAIRS
K·86

LAZY LIONS
LOUNGING
IN THE
LOCAL
LIBRARY
LASSIE COME HOME
LASSIE COME HOME
Lear
THE LEOPARD
LIMERICKS

LAW
LEMMINGS
Lions!
LORETTA LIPTON
LET'S LEARN LATIN
Leonardo
LEVITATION
Lady Chatterly's Lover
John Locke
LACROSSE
LOVE'S LABOURS LOST
LUKE
LIVING LEGENDS
LUXEMBOU
LITTLE BOY LOST

?123+= METICULOUS MICE MONITORING MYSTERIOUS MATHEMATICAL MESSAGES

Nine Nautical Newts
Navigating
Near Norway
NORTHERN STAR
ONE
OUTRAGEOUS
OLD
OSTRICH
ORDERING
AN
ONION
OMELETTE
Menu

Proud Peacocks
Preening
Perfect
Plumage

Peter Piper
VOTE
1
ME

Quivering Quails Queuing Quietly for Quills
Quills
Quality Quills
QUIZ
1 QUART
QUESTIONNAIRE
RALPH'S RENT-A

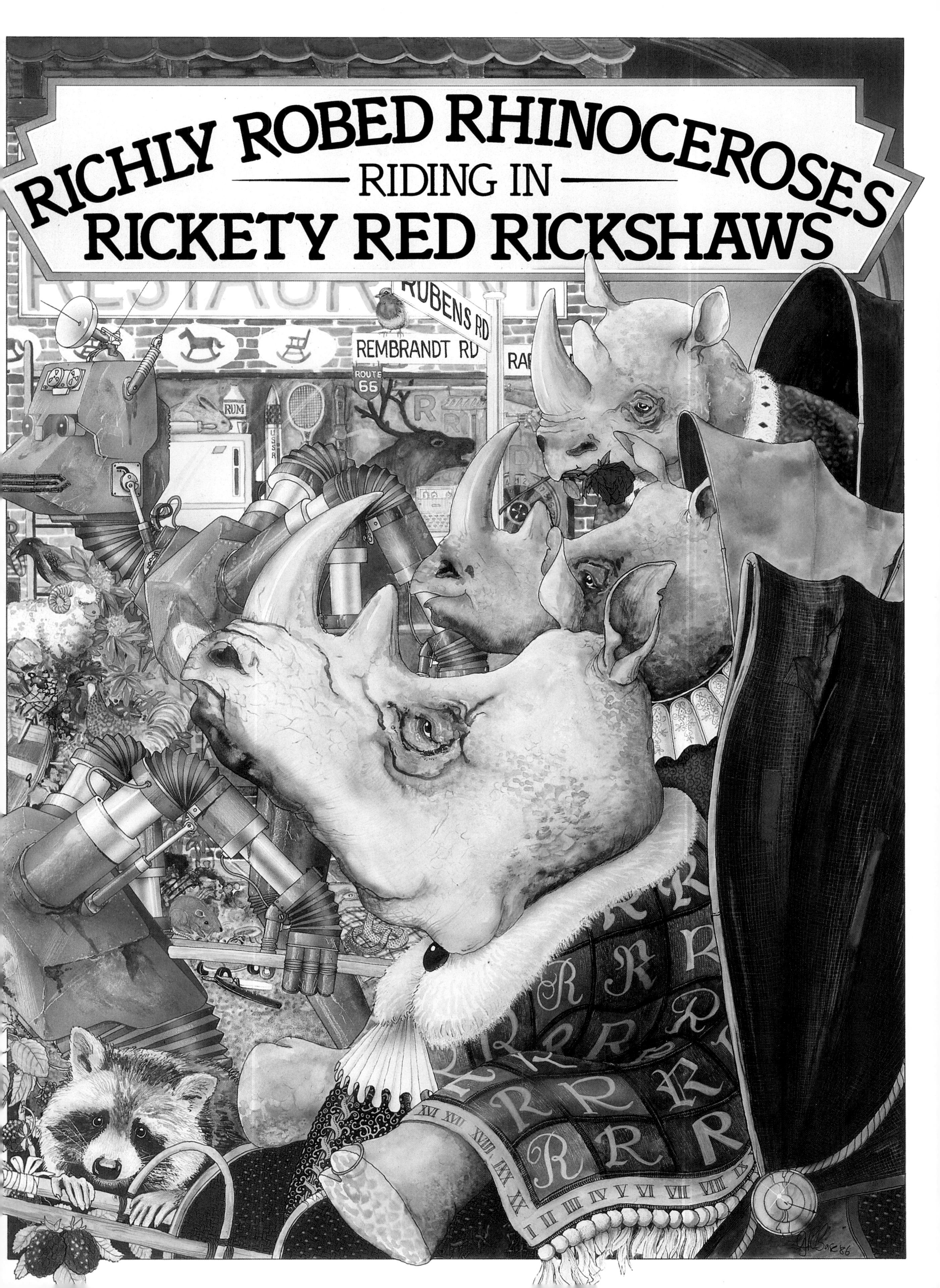
RICHLY ROBED RHINOCEROSES
RIDING IN
RICKETY RED RICKSHAWS
RUBENS RD
REMBRANDT RD
ROUTE 66
RUM

SIX · SLITHERING · SNAKES
SLIDING · SILENTLY · SOUTHWARD ·
SIX · SI
AKES
SLIDING · SILENTLY · SOUTHWARD ·
766-677-76-7=
STOP

TWO TIGERS
TAKING THE 10.20 TRAIN
TO TIMBUKTU
TICKETS
TIME TABLE
THISTLE THEATRE
TARZAN AND THE TOMB OF TUTANKHAMEN
CAST OF THOUSANDS
TONIGHT
the TOUCAN TAVERN
THE TERRACE TEA-ROOM
TOILETS
THE TIMBUKTU TORPEDO
TRANS TANZANI

UNRULY UNICORNS UPENDING URNS OF ULTRAMARINE UMBRELLAS

VICTOR V. VULTURE
THE
VAUDEVILLE
VENTRILOQUIST
VERSATILE
VIRTUOSO
OF
VOCIFEROUS
VERBOSITY
VEXATIOUSLY
VOCALIZING
AT
THE
VALHALLA
VARIETY
VENUE
VIOLET
Viscount

Wicked Warrior WASPS wildly waving Warlike Weapons

REX
FOX
FIXING
SIX
SAX
PHONES
SERVICE
GOOD LUCK, REX. XXX

Y1
2
S.S. YOGHURT
YOUTHFUL YAKS YODELLING
IN YELLOW YACHTS

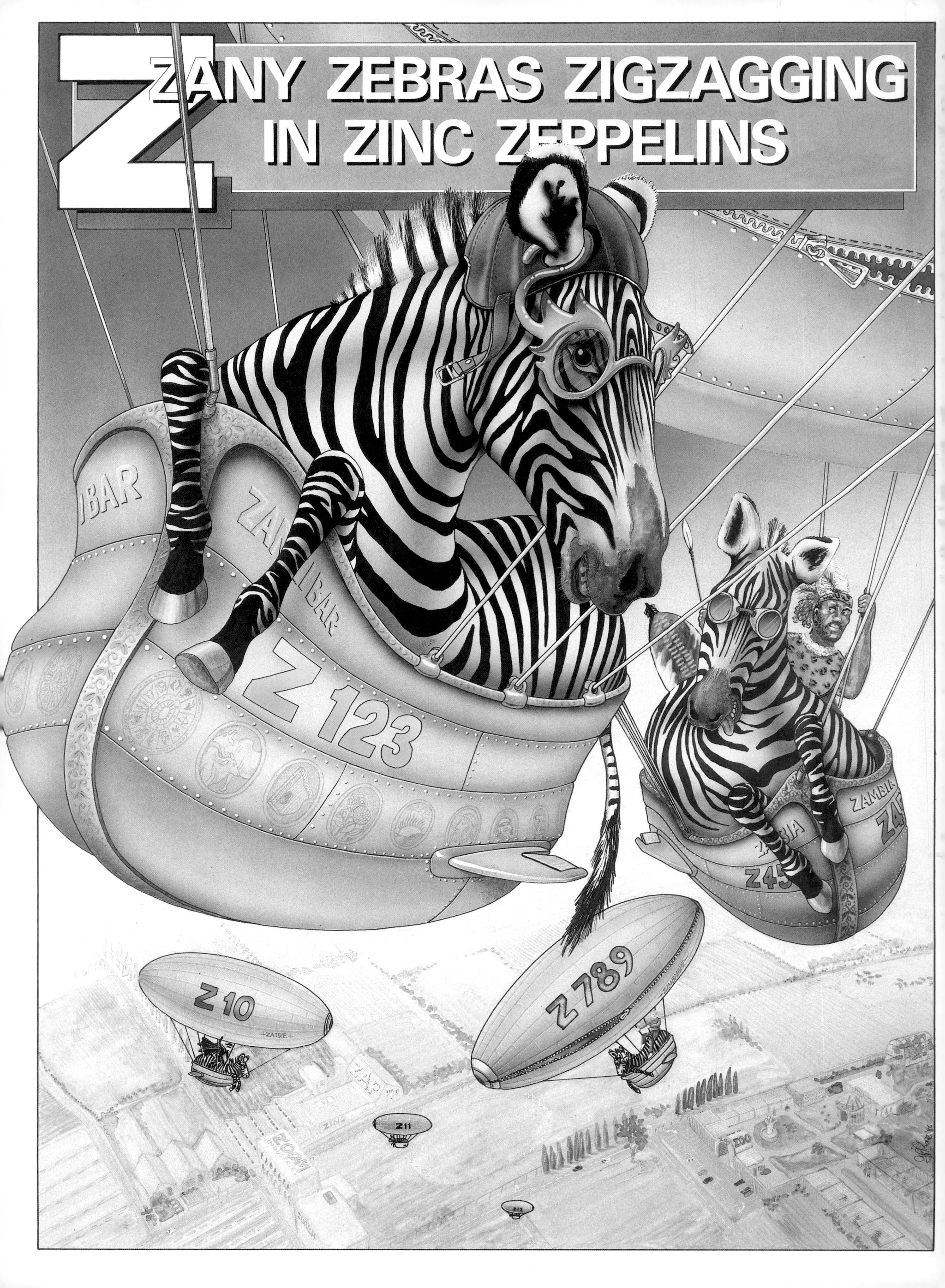
Z
ZANY ZEBRAS ZIGZAGGING
IN ZINC ZEPPELINS
Z 123
ZAMBIA
Z 789
Z 10
ZAIRE
ZAP
Z11
ZOO